W9-BYF-550

The Squirrel's Birthday
and Other Parties

The Squirrel's Birthday and Other Parties

STORIES BY

Toon Tellegen

ILLUSTRATED BY

Jessica Ahlberg

TRANSLATED BY

Martin Cleaver

BOXER BOOKS

Introduction

Toon Tellegen first began to invent animal stories to tell his daughter at bedtime. Then, when his daughter grew older, he decided to write them down. He created a world where there is only one forest, one river, one ocean, and one oak tree; a world of imagination where anything is possible. Toon has been writing stories about the squirrel, the ant, and the other animals in the forest for over 25 years, and to date more than 300 of them have been published in his native Holland. His work has been translated into many different languages and enjoyed by children all over the world. *The Squirrel's Birthday and Other Parties*, and its companion, *Letters to Anyone and Everyone*, are the first titles in a new series.

Contents

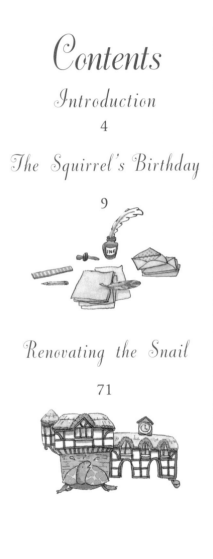

The
Squirrel's Birthday

To make sure that he never forgot anything, the squirrel had pinned little notes on the walls of his house.

On one such note was written
"Beechnuts."

The squirrel often read that note and said to himself, "Oh yes, beechnuts. I mustn't forget those."

Then he turned around, walked over to the cupboard, and soon afterward he was sitting enjoying a plate of beechnuts, sweet or stewed.

Another note simply stated,

"The ant."

When he chanced upon that particular note, the squirrel nodded and thought, "That's true, I really should go and see the ant."

Then he slid down the
beech trunk and walked over
to the ant's house, calling,
"Ant! Ant!" along the way.
Not long after, they were
sitting in the grass on the
riverbank, chatting about
things you could never
forget, and never remember.
They often sat there for hours.

On another note on the
squirrel's wall was written
"Be cheerful."

The squirrel sighed when he read that note. He did his best to be as cheerful as possible, but if he wasn't *feeling* cheerful, it was very hard to *make* himself cheerful. The ant had occasionally explained how to do it, but it had been a long and complicated story, a story the squirrel had not understood.

It was a strange note, the squirrel thought, but he didn't take it down from the wall.

In a back corner, where the squirrel hardly ever ventured, there was another note. It was hanging so far away that the squirrel only read it once a year. That note read, "My birthday."

One morning after he had read
the note saying "Beechnuts" twice
and frowned at the one stating
"Be cheerful," the squirrel saw this
remote note.

"My birthday," he read.

He slapped his forehead,
squeezed his eyes shut, and said,
"It's true! It's nearly my birthday!"

His heart thudded.

The squirrel went out of his
front door and sat down on the
log outside his house. It was still
early in the morning. The sun was
shining and the thrush was singing
in the distance.

The squirrel took a piece of beech bark and wrote:

Dear Ant,
Will you come to my birthday?
It's the day after tomorrow.
                    The squirrel.

Then he wrote on another piece of beech bark: *Dear Elephant.* Then: *Dear Whale,* and *Dear Earthworm.* "I want everyone to come," he thought, "and I mean everyone."

He wrote for hours, and by the afternoon there were piles of letters in front of him, and behind him, and beside him. They stretched up above his roof.

He kept thinking he'd invited everyone, but then he remembered someone else. *Dear Hummingbird*, he wrote, or *Dear Arctic Fox*, or *Dear Seahorse*.

By sunset, the squirrel couldn't think of anyone else. He racked his brain and wrote another letter, to the grasshopper. Then he thought again and said to himself, "Now I really can't think of anyone else."

Then the wind rose and blew the letters up in the air. The sky turned very dark and the wind rustled and swished around the squirrel.

The letters flew around in circles and
blew over the woods in all directions.

Soon the letters started to come down again. They swooped into the river, to the pike and the carp and the stickleback. Others bored their way into the ground, to the mole and the earthworm and the other animals that lived there. Some flew over the woods to the desert, to the camel and the sandfly, and others to the ocean, to the whale and the porpoise and the sea lion and the dolphin.

The squirrel took a deep breath and went into his house. "They're all sure to come," he thought. He glanced

18

at the note with "Beechnuts" on his wall and then said softly to himself, "Oh yes, beechnuts. I mustn't forget that. I'm hungry."

When he had finished two bowls of sweet beechnuts, he got into bed and thought one more time, "They're all sure to come." Then he snuggled up in his blanket and fell asleep.

Next
morning,
the answers
were
delivered
to the
squirrel.
There
were
more
letters
than he
could
count.

The squirrel sat on the branch outside his door and the letters piled up in front of him, beside him, and behind him. He opened them one by one, every time saying to himself, "I wonder who this letter is from," and then he read:

Dear Squirrel, Yes.

The ant.

Dear Squirrel, Yes.

The grasshopper.

Dear Squirrel, Yes.

The whale.

As he read each letter, the squirrel thought, "Goodness, so he's coming too; well I never!" Then he rubbed his hands in delight.

After a while, he had to stand on tiptoe to see beyond the letters, and later he had to dig a tunnel through them to reach some sunlight so he could read.

Some of the animals couldn't write or had forgotten how to write "Yes." Instead, they called, roared, cheeped, or squeaked "Yes." Their voices came from all directions.

The lobster considered himself far too distinguished to write and so he asked the lark to chirp "Yes" on his behalf. The lark ascended and jubilantly chirped on high in the blue sky, "Yes, says the lobster!

And me too! The lark!"

No one wrote "No" or called "No."

When darkness fell, the wind dropped and no more letters were delivered. Then the squirrel thought, "They'll all come."

Yet he had the feeling that he was still one answer short. But whose answer could it be?

He squeezed his eyes shut and thought, "Who can it be?" He really had no idea.

But then, in the dusk, a little note wafted in. It seemed to reflect the light, or to flash on and off.

It was the firefly signaling that he would be coming, too.

The squirrel read it, nodded, and thought, "Now I'm sure everyone is coming."

He went into his house, came across the note with "Beechnuts" written on it, said, "Oh yes, that's true," and had a large plate of hot, stewed beechnuts.

Then he sat down at his window in the dark and looked outside. "I can't sleep," he thought. He looked at the stars, and the little clouds floating by, and at the dark treetops.

That evening, the animals made their gifts for the squirrel.

They did so quietly and underwater, or deep in the bushes, or high above the clouds, because they wanted to surprise the squirrel.

Everyone made a gift.

The world rustled and shook, but very quietly, so that the squirrel, sitting in the dark by his window, thought it was so silent everywhere that he could only hear his heart beating.

"Will they really all come?" he wondered. Would they enjoy his birthday, or might it get a little boring? "That's possible," he thought. "You never know." Wrinkles of doubt appeared on his forehead. But then he shook his head and thought, "No, it'll never be boring, not if everyone comes. That's impossible."

He sat there for hours, until he fell asleep. Then he slowly slid off the chair and onto the floor, sleepwalked to his bed, and pulled the blanket over himself.

 In the meantime, the
animals were making gifts.

Big gifts and tiny gifts, red gifts
and blue gifts, gifts that
squeaked, and gifts that were
hot, or even very cold. They
made heavy gifts that took
ten of them to lift, and light
gifts they had to hold tight
so they wouldn't be blown
away by a gust of wind.

They made crooked gifts and thin
gifts that were dead straight, round
gifts that could roll and rough gifts

impossible
to push.

28

Gifts of wood,
gifts of honey,
and gifts of air,
gifts to eat and
gifts to put on
your head in
wintertime, or
on your tail
when it was
very cold.
Just about any
gift you could
think of, someone
had made it.

29

"It's almost his birthday," the
animals thought as they worked.
"Almost . . ." If they could quack or
sing, they quacked or sang softly,
"Almost, almost, oh almost . . ."

On the morning of his birthday,
the squirrel baked cakes. He was hard
at work even before the sun came up.

He wanted to bake so many cakes
that by the end of the day everyone would say, "I've had more than
enough to eat." "Only then would it
be a real birthday," he thought.

He baked huge honey cakes for the

bear and the bumblebee, a grass cake for the hippo, a small red cake for the mosquito, and a dry cake for the dromedary. He baked heavy salt cakes for the shark and the squid, and lowered them on a chain into the river. He baked thin cakes as light as air for the swallow and the wild goose and the oystercatcher, cakes so light they floated high above the trees on strings so they wouldn't fly away. He baked thick, moist cakes that were so heavy they could sink through the ground so the earthworm and the mole could eat them in the dark—which is where those cakes tasted best.

Occasionally the squirrel took a brief break, but not for long. Because countless cakes is a lot of cakes.

He baked a rough bark cake for the elephant and a small, moldy willow cake for the woodworm.
He thought deeply and then baked a cake made only of water for the dragonfly. It was a strange, gleaming cake and he put it to one side under the twigs of the rosebush.

He spent all morning baking and only finished when the sun was high in the sky and the party was about to begin. He looked around and nodded.

There were cakes everywhere—lying,
floating, standing, and hanging.
There were black cakes, white cakes,
lopsided cakes, spherical cakes,
tall cakes, and enormous,
clumsy cakes that slowly
disappeared into the ground.
Most of the cakes were still
steaming and spreading
a sweet scent. They
seemed to be
glistening with
impatience.

It was a warm,
sunny day in
midsummer.
There was
a cake for
everyone.

While the squirrel was baking cakes, the animals were choosing which clothes to wear to the party.

The elephant put on a small red jacket he had never worn before. The bear wore a large gray coat that was so baggy he couldn't possibly burst out of its seams. The mole looked for something that wasn't black, but he couldn't find anything,

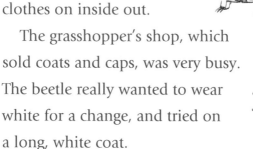

so he just put all his clothes on inside out.

The grasshopper's shop, which sold coats and caps, was very busy. The beetle really wanted to wear white for a change, and tried on a long, white coat.

The lizard put a purple cap
on the back of his head, and the
cricket asked if he could wear a large
red coat back to front, with a row of
golden buttons down his back.

"You can!" chirped the
grasshopper. "You can!"

In the ocean, the squid wrapped himself in a purple costume with dozens of sleeves through which he stuck his tentacles, the whale put a green pointed hat on his blowhole, and the walrus tied a small, yellow bow tie around his neck.

"Why not?" he thought.

Everyone chose something special to wear. Nobody wanted to go just the way they were.

Even the tortoise had
put on a bright red vest
over his shell, and the hedgehog
 put a blue sleeve over every
needle on his back.
It took him hours—
even longer than the slug,
who wormed his way into
a ramshackle shed
he had been given
long ago.

"I'm going to look
like no one has ever looked before,"
everyone thought.

Noon came. The sun was shining. "It's a beautiful day to celebrate a birthday," the animals thought. And everyone set off for the heart of the woods, for the clearing not far from the beech tree, beside the bend in the river, where the squirrel wanted to celebrate his birthday.

Meanwhile, the squirrel stood among his cakes in the open space in the woods.

No one had turned up.

Somber thoughts entered his head just for a moment. "Is it possible that they have forgotten it's my birthday?" he wondered. "Or maybe they don't remember where I live?

And the day after tomorrow, do they know what the day after tomorrow is? Or might they think that the day after tomorrow is always the day after tomorrow? Then I would only be having my birthday the day after tomorrow. But the day after tomorrow, my birthday would still be the day after tomorrow." It made him feel dizzy.

"Or maybe they changed their mind at the last moment," he thought. "Could they possibly be thinking, 'Oh, the squirrel! He won't have much of a birthday party'?"

A shadow crossed his face.

Just then, he saw the bear lumber toward him.

"Am I your first guest?" the bear called from a distance in his huge, baggy coat. "Yes," the squirrel called back.

"What kind of cakes do you have?" asked the bear.

"Lots of them," said the squirrel. "Just look."

Behind the bear came the cricket, and behind him the elephant and the beetle. The swan and the heron swooped down from the sky, followed by the thrush.

In the river, the pike stuck his head out of the water, and beside him the salmon leaped in the air, while the walrus looked around in surprise

and felt to make sure that his bow tie
was straight.

"Is it here?" he asked.

"Yes. It's here, Walrus. Here!" the
squirrel called cheerfully.

It wasn't long before a long
meandering line of animals, weighed
down with gifts, came through the
woods, across the blue sky, out of the
gleaming water, and up from the
black earth to visit the squirrel.

One by one, the animals gave
their best wishes to the squirrel
along with their gifts, as they sniffed
the scent of the countless cakes,
rubbed their hands, wings, and fins,
and looked around to see whether

43

everyone was looking at them and thinking, "Doesn't he look special? Goodness, I've never seen anyone so special."

Everyone looked special, and everyone was cheerful and looking forward to cake.

This is how the squirrel's birthday party started.

When all the animals had arrived, the squirrel cleared his throat and asked, "Would everyone like a piece of cake?"

"Yes!" they all called.

Soon they were all sitting and eating their favorite cake.

The woods fell still, but at the same time it was noisy, because there weren't many animals who could eat quietly. Most of them gulped and slurped, and muttered and growled with every mouthful.

Some kept choking, or swelled up, fell over, and still kept eating.

 Water splashed from the river, and occasionally pieces of algae cake floated to the surface, then disappeared a moment later into the mouth of the pike or the stickleback.

The mole regularly stuck his head out of the earth, took a deep breath, and said, "Delicious, Squirrel . . . and the earthworm agrees!" and disappeared again under the ground.

The swan pushed an elegant white cake in front of him, occasionally stuck his beak in, shook his head with amazement at such a delicacy, then pushed the cake further.

 The dragonfly
walked over his cake and sipped
a blissful little morsel now and then.

The elephant dropped pieces of
sweet bark around him, and the bear
only emerged from an enormous
honey cake after a long time, when
he had become fatter than the
remains of the cake.

"Delicious" was muttered,
and "Tasty," and "Scrumptious,"
and "Goodness."

They ate for hours and hours, until everyone fell over, slipped to the ground to lie on his back in the grass, or rest on the bed of the river. And there were still half and whole cakes everywhere.

"I've had more than enough to eat," they muttered and groaned.

The squirrel looked around him, satisfied. So there was enough for everyone after all.

After they had all been lying there like that for a while and doing their very best not to think about cake, the elephant jumped up and said, "Are we going to dance? What do you think? We have to dance, don't we?"

"That's true," said the giraffe. He stood up and went over to the elephant.

At the foot of the oak tree, on the warm, thick moss, the elephant and the giraffe put an arm on each other's shoulder and started dancing.

"This really is dancing,
Giraffe," said the elephant
after two steps.

"Yes," said the giraffe
and nodded with
his head on the
elephant's neck.

Soon afterward, the sun set and the moon rose large and red above the river. All the animals danced: the beetle with the bug, the tortoise with the slug, the cricket with the frog, the ostrich with the heron, and, occasionally treading on each other's toes, the hippo with the rhinoceros.

Underwater, the pike and the carp danced. The bumblebee and the butterfly danced in the rosebush, the swallow and the stork danced high in the sky, while the ant and the squirrel danced at the foot of the beech tree.

The thrush, the blackbird, and the nightingale sang a song on a branch in the middle of the beech tree, and the woodpecker pecked in time high up near the top. But they danced too, from one foot to the other, as they sang and pecked.

Far away at sea, where they'd gone to catch a breath of fresh air, the flying fish and the skate danced.

They jumped high above the water, turned, and splashed gracefully back into the waves.

Under the ground, between the roots of the beech tree, the mole and the earthworm danced.

The ground rumbled and shook from their strange steps.

All the animals danced.

They danced cheerfully and quickly, and occasionally slowly and seriously, and some animals even sobbed as they danced, without knowing why, because really they were very happy.

They danced like that for hours.

Late in the evening, all the animals went home. "Thank you very much, Squirrel," they said.

"Did you enjoy the party?" the squirrel asked.

"Yes," they said. "It was lovely."

Everyone was tired and had to shuffle and drag themselves forward.

Some could hardly get off the ground. The mole slowly descended deep underground, and the woodworm managed to crawl into an old piece of wood with great difficulty.

The pike swam off and so did the walrus—even though he didn't know where to. "I never do," he thought. His yellow bow tie was hanging loose around his neck.

The glowworm didn't glow anymore, and the hippo yawned, stretched, and disappeared in the undergrowth.

The bear took one last good look around to see whether there were any crumbs of honey cake left. When he found a crumb, he closed his eyes, imagined it was an enormous honey cake, opened his mouth wide, and threw the crumb inside. "Ah," he muttered, "delicious. A little small, but delicious."

Finally he went home too.

"Goodbye, Squirrel," the ant said. He was the last to leave.

"Goodbye, Ant," said the squirrel.

"I think I'll be going," said the ant.

The squirrel nodded. He didn't know if the ant was going to say anything else. He saw him disappear slowly behind the oak tree.

The moon shone high above the woods and the river glistened. It was very quiet.

The squirrel sat under the beech tree in the moonlight, surrounded by his gifts.

"It was a beautiful birthday,"
he thought. "I think I'm very happy."

He sat there like that for a while,
by himself, in the silent wood. The
mist crept low over the ground and
wrapped itself around the bushes.

Then the squirrel climbed up
into the beech tree with piles
of gifts under his arms and
on his back.

He had difficulty getting through his front door.

"Did everything go well?" he wondered. "Was there really enough of every kind of cake for everyone? Wasn't there anyone I forgot? Or anything?"

He put down his gifts. "Can it be that someone wasn't satisfied?" he wondered. "The rhinoceros maybe? Or the slug? Had the slug enjoyed himself? Could it be that someone was getting into bed right now, thinking, 'That birthday wasn't up to much'?"

"I think everyone was pleased," he thought to himself.

The whole room was full of gifts. He looked around and saw the note that said "Beechnuts." However, he didn't go to his cupboard, but took the note off the wall and put it in the table drawer. "I'll put it away for a while," he thought.

He looked around again and then sat on the edge of the table and swung his feet back and forth.

Suddenly it was as if he felt sad. "But that's impossible!" he thought. After all, there was nothing to be sad about.

This wasn't sadness. This was something else. But he didn't know what.

Then he heard the voice of the ant far below him. "Squirrel!"

The squirrel walked over to his window, opened it, and looked down.

"Hello, Ant!" he called.

The ant was standing at the foot of the beech tree and looking up. He waved. It looked as if he didn't really know why he was standing there.

"I just wanted to say it was a nice party," he said hesitantly.

"Yes," said the squirrel.

"Very nice," said the ant.

"Yes."

There was a brief silence.

The ant rubbed his feet on the ground. "I couldn't sleep," he said.

"No," said the squirrel. He wondered briefly whether he should offer the ant anything, perhaps something sweet. But it didn't strike him as a good idea.

"Couldn't you sleep either?" asked the ant.

"No," said the squirrel.

It was quiet again.

"I'd better be getting home," the ant continued. "But it really was a very nice party, Squirrel."

"Yes," said the squirrel.

"Bye," said the ant.

"Bye, Ant," said the squirrel, and he saw the ant walk away in the darkness, very slowly, rocking slightly from one foot to the other.

"He is preoccupied," the squirrel thought. "I can see that."

He also felt a different kind of feeling he wasn't yet familiar with, one like nothing else. "This is a strange feeling," he thought, amazed.

Then he shrugged his shoulders, sighed, pushed his gifts aside, and got into bed.

When the squirrel had fallen asleep, the moon set and the night crept through the wood.

He rustled in the bushes and sometimes blew briefly against the leaves on the trees. Under the beech tree, the night stumbled over the gifts that the squirrel had not yet been able to take up with him.

Some were not even unwrapped yet, and lay there gleaming in the light of the inquisitive stars.

The night strolled on dreamily across the empty clearing where the animals had danced. But now it had fallen silent and the first drops of dew were hanging on the blades of grass.

He walked light-footedly, but occasionally he suddenly stamped. He stamped in front of the door of the slug, who was sleeping deeply and sluggishly, and he stamped on the ground above the head of the mole, so the mole dreamed of underground thunder and collapses, and then of sweet darkness again.

When he reached the river, the
night stepped onto the water. He
strode over the waves and made them
splash under his feet between the
reeds, making the frog briefly start
awake, croak something
incomprehensible, and
then fall asleep again,
as the pike looked up
with sleepy eyes and
thought, "The night."

On the other bank,
the night whispered to the
glowworm, who was sitting in the
blackberry bush, "Sl . . . sleep on . . ."
And the glowworm slept and didn't
light up.

The night crept through the woods, after the squirrel's birthday, and made everyone dream and then awaken briefly before falling asleep again.

From time to time, the night growled, but not wickedly.

And when the sun started to rise just below the horizon, against the low-hanging clouds, and the first rays of pink and orange appeared in the sky, the night faded and disappeared.

And everyone slept on.

Renovating
the Snail

In the morning, when I wake up," the snail said, "I always have such a pain in my horns."

"Oh really?" said the giraffe. "That's funny! So do I. It's as if they're prickling."

"Yes," said the snail. "As if they're on fire."

"As if someone is pulling hard at them," said the giraffe.

"Yes," said the snail. "That's what the pain is like."

They nodded at each other and felt pleased that they shared a morning complaint.

"Of course," said the giraffe, "I can't discuss such things with the sparrow."

"No," said the snail. "Or with the tortoise. But I can talk to him about renovation."

"Renovation?" asked the giraffe. "What's that?" And he gazed quizzically at the snail.

"Well . . ." said the snail slowly, weighing his words, "it's very difficult to explain."

The giraffe tried to think of something that was difficult to explain too, but he couldn't come up with anything at such short notice. He muttered something grumpily under his breath, and then walked off.

The snail had recently
had a long chat with
the tortoise. They both found
their accommodation
too cramped. It was
worst when they had
guests and it was
raining. The tortoise wanted
a shed with a lean-to. "But how can
I drag that around?" he wondered.
"Maybe I could add a wing
on one side." That struck
him as a nice idea.

The snail was
more interested
in an extra floor.

That morning, after talking
to the giraffe, he decided to start
work on the renovation at once.

It was still nice and early
and he only wanted one extra
floor. By the end of the afternoon,
the floor was finished. There was
even a small balcony on the front.
"That is for when I want to see
someone approaching from
a distance," the snail said
to himself, and felt
very satisfied.

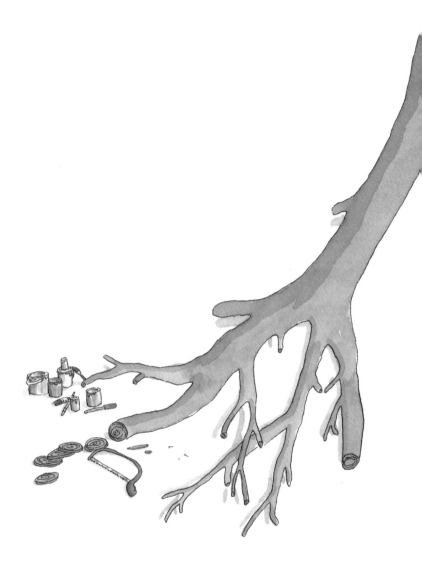

In the evening, the snail threw
a party to celebrate his renovation
work. One by one, the animals were
allowed to stand on the balcony and
wave at the others down below.

"Hello!" the others called up to
them.

Toward the end of the evening,
the giraffe stepped out onto the
balcony. He leaned a long way
forward and his neck almost reached
the ground. He beckoned to the
flamingo.

"Shall we talk about dancing?"

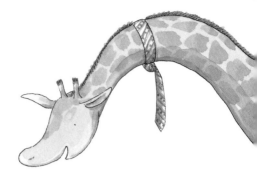

he asked loudly. "I never get an opportunity to discuss that with anyone, and it's so difficult to explain."

But the snail didn't hear him. He was just closing the door behind him on the lower floor. "No one ever needs to come down here again," he thought to himself, satisfied. "I can really live on my own down here."

And while the party went on noisily outside, the snail climbed into bed and went to sleep.

A Speck of Dust

At the edge of the woods, under
the rosebush, the bumblebee had
a shop. It was only a small shop,
without a window or even a counter,
but there were lots of things for sale.
There were things hardly anyone ever
needed: a pine needle, a ball of fluff,
a drop of water, a blade of grass,
a piece of beech bark, and a wilting
willow herb.

"Sometimes," was the answer the
bumblebee gave when anybody asked
him if he ever sold anything.

One day, the leopard gave
a party. He invited only the most
distinguished of animals; he didn't

ask the cockroach or the earthworm
or the hornet, nor did he invite the
hippopotamus, the squirrel, or the
ant. But he did ask the wasp, the
swan, the cobra, the flamingo, the

trout, and the grasshopper.

On the day of the party,
the grasshopper stood in front
of his mirror and examined
his appearance carefully.
Did he look distinguished enough?

He pulled the lapels of his jacket
closer together, pushed his shoulders
back a little, polished his antennae
yet again, and allowed
a distinguished smile
to cross his lips.

"And yet," he thought, as he imagined how he would enter the leopard's house, "something is still missing, something distinguished, something . . ."

Suddenly he knew what it was. He looked around, opened drawers, jumped on cabinets, peered into vases,

and ran his finger along ledges. But he couldn't find what he was looking for.

He hurried outside and
asked the swallow, who had
been invited at the last minute
and was ironing his jacket.
But the swallow couldn't
help him either. The
grasshopper ran to the
bumblebee's shop.

He stumbled inside, panting.

"I need a speck of dust," he said.
His antennae quivered, he
was so flustered.

"A speck of dust . . ." the
bumblebee said thoughtfully.
"I think I still have one of those."

He led the grasshopper to a
corner of the shop where a small
gray speck of dust lay behind
a sign that said NO COUGHING.

The grasshopper looked at
the speck of dust closely and
said, "I'd really prefer a slightly
paler speck of dust, but this will do.
How much do I owe you?"

"Let me see . . ." said the bumblebee. "That will be a fortune."

The grasshopper regretted not knowing how much a fortune was. On top of that, he didn't have anything with him. "But," he thought, "this evening I shall meet so many prominent animals that there must be someone with a couple of fortunes who won't mind giving one to me."

"Tomorrow morning I shall give you a fortune," he said.

"That's fine by me," said the bumblebee, and he flew up to the ceiling and back down again with delight.

The grasshopper picked up the speck of dust and left the shop.

That evening he entered
the hall where the leopard
was giving his party.
He stopped briefly in
the doorway and looked
around the assembled
company. He saw the
flamingo, who was gazing out of
a window in a civilized fashion;
the gazelle, who fanned
his forehead with an aspen
leaf; and the swan, who was
doing his very best to look
deep in thought.

The leopard broke off his
conversation with the red deer
and walked over to the grasshopper.

"Grasshopper!" he said. "Welcome.
Welcome." He extended one of his
claws hospitably. The grasshopper
nodded almost imperceptibly. At the
same time, he tilted his head slightly
to one side. Then, with an airy
gesture, he brushed the speck of dust
from his shoulder, as he smiled
mildly and engagingly.

The Rhinoceros's Wish List

One day, the cricket opened
a shop for wish lists, because most
animals don't know what they want
for their birthday.

The cricket sat on a chair behind
the counter and eagerly rubbed his
hands together, waiting for his first
customer.

It turned out to be the rhinoceros.
His birthday was in the coming week
and he had no idea what
he wanted.

"Aha!" said the cricket.

He took a piece of paper and wrote:

The rhinoceros's wish list

Then he emerged from behind the counter, walked around the rhinoceros a few times, muttered to himself, lifted one of the rhinoceros's ears, looked behind it, and walked back again.

On the wish list, he wrote:

One grass cake

"One grass cake?" asked the rhinoceros.

"Yes," said the cricket. "You'll get that from me. Made of stringy grass with buttercups and sweet clover."

"Great," said the rhinoceros. "And with a few thistles in it, please."

The cricket thought deeply and at length, squeezed his eyes shut, cleared his throat, and then wrote on the list:

All kinds of things

"What's that?" asked the rhinoceros.

"Don't you know?" asked the cricket.

"No," said the rhinoceros.

"Well," said the cricket, "then it's absolutely perfect. Because you can't know. That's why it's called 'all kinds of things'."

He jumped up and down with pleasure, and his jacket flapped all around him.

The rhinoceros took the wish list with him and showed it to everyone. The grass cake was crossed out, because he was already getting that.

One week later, on his birthday, the rhinoceros got a grass cake with thistles from the cricket, and from the other animals he got all kinds of things, and that made him very happy.

A Cake for Someone Who Doesn't Feel Like Cake

One day, the squirrel was walking along the edge of the woods when he saw a cake standing among the lilacs.

"A cake," he thought, "where you'd least expect it on an everyday morning. I really like that!" He walked around the cake. It was a beechnut cake with cream and red sugar. A sweet scent wafted toward the squirrel. "Who can it belong to?" he wondered. Then he noticed that there was a card on the cake:

*This cake is
for someone
who doesn't
feel like cake.*

"Oh," thought
the squirrel,
"that is a pity."
He sighed deeply,
hesitated briefly,
and said to him-
self, "No. No."
Then he sighed
again and
walked away.

He looked back a couple of times. The cake seemed to glow among the lilac bushes.

"Why do I always, always feel like cake?" wondered the squirrel.

As he walked, he thought about how he could make sure he didn't feel like cake.

"But if I don't feel like cake," he thought to himself, "then I don't feel like cake."

It made him feel dizzy, and he decided to think about something else. "The river!" he thought. The squirrel thought as quickly as he could about the river, the water in the river, the waves on the river, the babbling of the river, and the gleaming of the river. He sat down on the grass. The river was in front of him.

Soon the carp stuck his head above
the water and started a conversation
with the squirrel about rain,
watercress, moonlight, and what
wet really was.

"Wet is nothing," said the carp.

The sun shone and the squirrel
listened. Suddenly he exclaimed,
"I don't feel like cake anymore!"

He jumped up and ran away.
The carp watched him
in amazement.

"Now I'll never know whether he
agrees with me or not," he muttered,
and dived underwater dejectedly.

The squirrel ran back toward the edge of the woods. But before he got there, he slowed his pace and sighed sadly. "I do feel like cake," he thought, "and there's nothing I can do about it."

He decided to go and look at the cake anyway. There he found the ant, who was walking around the cake with a somber face, occasionally taking a few steps backward, pinching his nose and storming up to the cake with his eyes shut. But just before he reached the cake, he would stop and shake his head.

"Hello, Ant," said the squirrel.

"This is a black day, Squirrel," said the ant, "a black day."

They stood a few paces away from the cake, silently sniffing the scent of honey and staring at the thick cream and sweet iced towers piled high on top of the cake.

"I can't bear to look at the cake anymore, Squirrel," said the ant, "and yet . . ."

"Let's leave," said the squirrel. "This cake isn't good for us."

"Yes," said the ant.

They walked away, deep in thought.

A moment later, they heard a loud slurping sound. Looking around, they saw the elephant taking large bites out of the cake.

"Didn't you read the card?"
the ant exclaimed, his voice trembling
and his legs shaking.

"Yes," said the elephant. "I don't really
want this cake at all. Beechnut cake—
awful. If there'd been some sweet tree
bark in it . . . but there wasn't. Just sugar
and beechnuts. Call that a cake?"

And without a trace of relish,
and occasionally emitting a grunt of
disgust, the elephant ate the cake, while
the ant and the squirrel watched from a
distance.

"Poor Elephant!" murmured the ant.

The squirrel almost called, "Enjoy
your meal!" But he changed his mind,
and didn't say a word.

The Whale
and the Seagull

Far away in the ocean, between a few rocks close to the bottom of a trough, lived the whale. He lay motionless in the deep water and gazed into the distance. He had the feeling that he shouldn't lose sight of something, but he had no idea what that something was. He had never closed his eyes, just in case.

He lay there all alone. He didn't get many visitors. When he thought about it, he didn't actually get any

visitors at all. No one had ever
been to see him. He didn't know
what *someone* would look like anyway.
On very odd occasions he sighed. Then
some sand was dislodged from the
ocean floor and the water around him
turned cloudy. He thought this was a
dangerous situation and said to himself,
"You can do anything you like, but don't
sigh, I beg you." Then years would
pass until he forgot, and sighed again.
"There you go again!" he would say to
himself, as grains of sand stung his eyes.

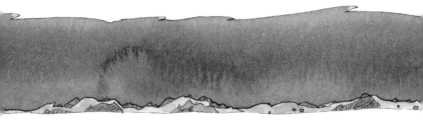

"What did I tell you?"

The whale was convinced he would lie there forever.

But one day, a note floated down through the ocean with a stone attached to it to make sure it sank. It lay there on the ocean floor in front of the whale. "What can that be?" the whale wondered. "A note! I've never seen one of those before. And I don't even know if I can read." He opened the note and discovered that he could read. He read:

Dear Whale,

I'm not sure if you exist, but I'm
inviting you to my party anyway.
Tomorrow on the beach. If you exist,
will you come?

The seagull

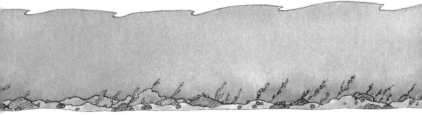

The whale was so surprised that he sighed deeply and briefly lost sight of the whole world. But he didn't mind, because he could only think about one thing. "A party!" he thought. "I'll meet *someone* there!" He wondered if he'd recognize *someone* if he saw them, and whether he should take anything with him or wear something special.

Just in front of him, to one side, was a piece of coral, red and gleaming. He thought *someone* might like that.

So he lodged it under a fin and started swimming toward the beach.

He looked around one more time. "I wonder if I'll ever come back here," he thought. He didn't know what a party was or how long it would last. "Maybe the party will never end," he thought. "You know what," he said to himself, "we'll just have to see."

And from the deepest depths of the ocean, he swam to the beach.

He arrived there early in the evening.

He stuck his head above the surf
and saw that the whole beach was
decorated with algae, seaweed and
shells, and other things he'd never seen
before. And he saw the moon, high
in the sky, and the stars. And for the
very first time, just for a moment, he
closed his eyes. He didn't know why.
Something rolled out, down his cheek.

"That's strange," he thought. "And
what is that thumping inside me?"

The seagull saw him.

"Whale!" he called. "It's you!"

He flapped over to him. "So that's
someone," the whale thought to himself.

114

The seagull accompanied him to the water's edge and settled him into a hollow. That evening the whale met the shark, the dogfish, and the skate; he saw the tern and the albatross and even the ant.

"I really must remember this," he thought, but he didn't know what for. In the middle of the night, the party reached its climax and the seagull asked the whale if he wanted to dance.

"Yes, please," said the whale.

115

They straightened their backs and
the whale rested a fin on the seagull's
shoulder, while the seagull draped a
wing around the whale's middle.

Then they danced, silently and
seriously, on the moon-drenched beach,
to the sound of the slow surf. Everyone
held their breath and thought: "No one
has ever danced like this before."

The seagull and the whale danced
right across the beach, to the dunes
and back again, along the water's edge,
and they finished their dance with
a jump so high they seemed
to disappear in the sky.

Then they flopped back down
onto the wet sand.

"Maybe," the whale thought,
"I'm happy now." As far as he was
concerned, time could stop right
there, that night, on the beach,
at the seagull's party.

The Set Table

One sunny morning, the squirrel and the ant took a stroll through the woods. As they walked, the ant explained to the squirrel why the sun shines and why the rain, when it falls, falls as drops and not as leaves. The squirrel nodded, occasionally said, "Yes," and meanwhile thought about other things.

Presently, they reached a part of the woods they didn't know very well.

"I *do* know where we are," said the ant.

"You know everything," said the squirrel.

"Almost," said the ant. "By the way, do you know why trees grow upward and not sideways? Sideways would be so much easier, wouldn't it?"

The squirrel didn't know and was surely about to find out, but just at that moment they happened upon a small, grassy clearing.

They didn't know the spot, nor did they know who lived there.

In the middle of the clearing was a large table set with plates and glasses and bowls of the most delicious food. Some of the dishes were steaming; others seemed to be fermenting, or had coils of sweet fragrance rising from them.

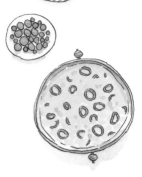

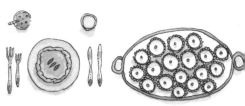

"Hmm!" said the ant,
and did his very best
to avoid sticking a finger
in one of the bowls
right then.

There was no sign
of anyone around.

"Hello!" called the
squirrel.

"Happy birthday!"
called the ant.

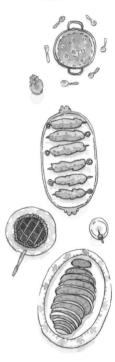

"Is anyone here?" asked the squirrel.

"Let's just dig in!" said the ant, who had caught sight of a cake made of granulated sugar. The squirrel stopped him just in time.

Not a breath of wind stirred the clearing. The sun shone, the sugar melted, and still no one appeared.

"I'll count to three," said the ant and immediately started counting.

"Hmm," said the squirrel, "I really don't know about this."

"Three," said the ant, who hadn't heard a word, and he began tasting everything.

It wasn't long before the squirrel took a bite too.

They sat
there feasting
for some time.
The sun was
already
starting
to set when they
finally stood up and
prepared to go home,
one step at a time.

Suddenly they heard
a voice: "Thank you both
very much."

They looked around.
Then they saw the dragonfly
sitting almost invisibly on
the branch of a bush.

125

"Oh, don't mind us," said the squirrel. The ant said nothing.

"You know," the dragonfly said, "I'm always afraid that I won't have enough, or that it'll be worthless— that's why I hide. If someone doesn't want anything or doesn't like it, well, then I'm just not there."

"Oh, Dragonfly," said the squirrel.

The dragonfly blushed and took a step backward.

"I'll celebrate the rest of my birth-day on my own," he said quickly.

"I'll come and bring you a present tomorrow," said the squirrel.

The ant had a little difficulty nodding.

"What would you like?"
asked the squirrel.

But the dragonfly had
already disappeared
behind a leaf of the bush,
early on the evening of
his birthday.

The Costume Party

Every so often, one of the animals would throw a grand party in the woods. Each time this happened, everyone would say that this would be the grandest party yet.

This time, the elephant was hosting the party and everyone had to wear a costume.

The squirrel thought for a long time and decided to go dressed as the ant. He knew the ant so well that he had no trouble looking exactly like him.

When he arrived for the party,
the elephant stopped him. "Ant, you
can only come in if you're wearing
a costume."

"But . . ."

"No. No buts. Go home and
make sure you put something
on so I can't recognize you.
Then you can come in.

"We have delicious
sugar sticks,
by the way . . ."

"Sugar sticks!" thought the squirrel,
and he went home, disappointed.
He stood in front of the mirror and
thought for a long time. Then he
decided to go as the wasp. He had
often sat beside the wasp on a branch
or accompanied him as he visited
a flower. And he had always admired
his beautiful yellow and black
outfit. "I have something
just like that," the squirrel thought.
Using a few beechnut shells and
some resin, he quickly made
a beautiful wasp suit.

But again he was sent away.

"Wasp," said the elephant, "you'll only be allowed in if you wear a costume. I have already sent the ant away. I can't make an exception for you."

"But . . ."

"That's what the ant said too. But it's no use. This is the grandest party ever and you can't ruin it by coming as yourself. Put something on. It doesn't matter what."

The squirrel walked home sadly. He didn't feel like going to the party anymore and, anyway, it was getting late and most of the tasty snacks would have been eaten by now.

In the distance, he could hear the drumming feet of the millipede. He suspected the earthworm would be dancing now, beside tables heavily laden with bowls of cake. He started walking faster and took off his wasp suit as he went. When he got home, he threw all the clothes in a corner, tied his tail around his waist, and stuck one ear over his eye with some resin. Then he went back to the party.

"Ah!" said the elephant. "Look what we have here . . . beautiful, beautiful. I don't even recognize you!"

The elephant stood wondering whether it was the ant or the wasp who had dressed up as the squirrel. Meanwhile, the squirrel dug into his first piece of cake and watched as the earthworm slid elegantly across the floor.

A
Little
Black Box

One evening, the
squirrel and the ant were sitting
side by side on the top branch
of the beech tree. It was hot and
quiet, and they gazed at the tops
of the trees and the stars. They
had eaten honey and talked about
the sun, the riverbank, letters, and
misgivings.

"I'm going to keep this evening,"
said the ant. "Do you mind?"

The squirrel gave him
a surprised look.

The ant took out a small
black box. "The thrush's birthday
is in here too," he said.

"The thrush's birthday?" asked
the squirrel.

"Yes," said the ant, and he took the birthday out of the box. And once again they ate sweet chestnut cake with elderberry cream and danced while the nightingale sang and the firefly flashed on and off, and they saw the beak of the thrush glisten with pleasure all over again. It was the most beautiful birthday they could remember.

The ant put the birthday back in the box.

"I'll put this evening in too," he said. "There's already a lot in there." He closed the box, said goodbye to the squirrel, and went home.

That night, the squirrel sat for a long time on the branch in front of his door and thought about the box. What would it be like in the box for this evening? Would it get squashed or faded? Would it still taste of honey? Would it always go back in after being taken out? Could it fall and break, or roll away?

And what else could be in
the box? Adventures the
ant had alone? Mornings in
the grass on the riverbank,
when the waves glistened?
Letters from distant animals?
Could it ever fill up, so that
nothing else would fit in?
And might there be other
boxes too, for sad days?

His head spun. He went
into his house and climbed
into bed.

By then, the ant was fast
asleep in his home under
the bush. The box was on
a shelf above his head.
But he hadn't closed it
tightly enough. In the
middle of the night, the box
suddenly shot open and an
old birthday flew out across
the room at high speed.
And all at once, the ant
was dancing with the
elephant in the moonlight
under the lime tree.

"But I'm asleep!" called the ant.

"Oh, never mind," said the elephant, and he whirled the ant round and round. He flapped his ears and trunk and said, "Aren't we dancing beautifully?" and, "Oh, pardon me," when he stepped on the ant's toes.

The glowworm glowed in the rosebush and the squirrel sat on the bottom branch of the lime tree and waved to the ant.

Suddenly, the birthday slipped back into the box, and a moment later, the ant woke up.

He rubbed his eyes and looked around. Bright moonlight fell through the window and onto the

little black box on the shelf. The ant
stood up and pushed the lid down
firmly. Then he held the box to his
ear and heard music and rustling
and the lapping of waves.
He even thought he heard the
taste of honey, though he
wasn't sure that was possible.

He frowned for a moment,
then got back into bed.

$\mathcal{R}$ead about another book
from Toon Tellegen . . .

$\mathcal{L}etters$ to
$\mathcal{A}nyone$
and
$\mathcal{E}veryone$

Dear Snail,
May I invite you to dance with
me on top of your house? Just a few
steps? That's what I want most of all.
I promise I'll dance very delicately,
so we won't fall through your roof.
But of course, you can never be
really sure.
The elephant

The elephant invites the snail to dance. The squirrel writes a letter to a table. The mole, all alone underground, writes letters to himself.

This collection of fantastic, dreamlike tales conjures up a world where the creatures of the earth can send a letter to the sun (and get an answer); where you can actually write a letter to a letter; and where just writing something down can make it true. This extraordinary correspondence between the animals and the world around them will capture the imaginations of adults and children alike.

About the Author

Toon Tellegen is one of
Holland's most celebrated writers
for both children and adults. He
started his literary career as a poet,
and began writing for children
in the mid-1980s. Toon lives in
Amsterdam, and loves reading,
telling stories, and huge, sweet cakes.

About the Illustrator

*J*essica Ahlberg studied at
Winchester School of Art and has
gone on to illustrate several books
for children. She likes, among other
things, writing letters, looking at
maps, reading books, doing home
improvements, and making cakes.
She lives in Brighton, England, and
loves walking by the ocean and
sometimes swimming in it.

For Molly
Toon Tellegen

For Johanna
Jessica Ahlberg

First American edition published in 2009
by Boxer Books Limited.

Distributed in the United States and Canada by
Sterling Publishing Co., Inc.
387 Park Avenue South, New York, NY 10016-8810

First published in Great Britain in 2009
by Boxer Books Limited
www.boxerbooks.com

Translated by Martin Cleaver

Edited by Frances Elks

Original English translation copyright © 2009 Boxer Books Limited

Book design by Amelia Edwards

Library of Congress Cataloging-in-Publication Data available.

ISBN 978-1-906250-93-5

1 3 5 7 9 10 8 6 4 2

Printed in Italy

All of our papers are sourced from managed forests
and renewable resources.